For information address Disney Press,
1101 Flower Street, Glendale, California 91201.

Printed in China
First Edition
1 3 5 7 9 10 8 6 4 2
ISBN 978-1-4847-0283-3
T425-2382-5-13338

For more Disney Press fun, visit www.disneybooks.com
This book was printed on paper created from a sustainable source.

Jasmine
and
the Star of Persia

DISNEP PRESS

New York • Los Angeles

Princess Jasmine loved the stars. But even more, she loved the stories Aladdin told her about them. Every night they would lie on the Magic Carpet and gaze up at the twinkling sky above them, and every night Aladdin would tell a different, wondrous tale.

"What about that star?" Jasmine asked one evening. "The violet one."

"Ah, that," said Aladdin, "is the Star of Persia . . . named after the legendary jewel—the biggest, most beautiful amethyst in the world."

"Jewel?" said Jasmine, her eyes wide with curiosity.

"According to the legend," Aladdin began, "the Star of Persia belonged to a beautiful queen who ruled a tiny kingdom many years ago. She was wise and fair and kind. Her subjects loved her dearly and lived in happiness and peace for all the years that she reigned.

"But alas," Aladdin said with a sigh, "not even great queens can live forever. When this good queen died, her subjects hid the jewel away, high in a tower, sure that there would never be one worthy of its beauty again."

Jasmine's eyes twinkled. "Tell me, is that story *true*?"

Aladdin shrugged. "I don't know. But there is one way to find out . . . if you really want to."

Jasmine smiled. "Of course I do!"

Early the next morning,
Jasmine, Aladdin, and their
monkey, Abu, set off on the
Magic Carpet. They flew east,
and before long, they were
soaring over a tiny kingdom.
A tall, imposing tower rose
from a central plaza.

"Look!" Jasmine called, peering over the edge of the Magic Carpet. "I wonder if that's where the queen's jewel is hidden."

"Let's fly down," said Aladdin. "We'll see if there's a way in."

But when they touched down, they discovered that the tower was even more imposing from the ground. Iron bars were on the windows and a thick chain was fastened around the door. It was clear that without a key (or at least a clever genie), there was little chance of getting in.

All of a sudden, the grumpy-looking guard standing next to the door spoke up. "What do you want?" he demanded.

Jasmine walked up to him and grinned. "We've heard about the Star of Persia," she explained, "and we've come to see the jewel."

"I'm afraid that's impossible," the guard said. "No one can see the jewel except a queen as lovely and worthy as our own."

"Ah," said Aladdin. "Well, allow me to introduce you to Princess Jasmine. She's not a queen yet, but she will be one day."

"Yes, yes," the guard said impatiently. "But our queen was very wise."

"I'm wise, too!" Jasmine declared.

"Oh, yes?" said the guard. He thought for a moment. "Then tell me—what is the square root of one hundred?"

Jasmine smiled. "That's easy. It's ten, of course!"

"That's correct," said the guard. Then his eyes narrowed. "But the answer is still no. After all, our queen was not only wise, she was fair, as well."

"*I'm* fair," Jasmine assured him.

The guard's eyes searched the plaza. "Fair enough to solve that argument over there?" he asked.

"Yes, I think so." Jasmine nodded and, after making her way across the plaza, proceeded to do just that.

"You did well," admitted the guard. "But the answer is still no. For our queen was not only wise and fair . . ." He paused for a moment to sniff and wipe away a tear. "She was also very kind."

"Ah," said Jasmine, placing her hand on his shoulder. "You still miss her, don't you?" Then she turned to Aladdin. "Let's not bother him anymore," she said. "I'll go get him a drink from that fountain over there. He must get thirsty standing in the sun all day. Then we'll be on our way."

Jasmine hurried to the fountain, which she was surprised to find quite dry. To her relief, however, as soon as she held a jar under it, a stream of cool, clear water came bubbling out.

Then, her jar full, she turned to take it to the guard—only to find him and most everyone else in the plaza gathered around her, staring.

"What?" she asked. "Did I do something wrong?"

"The fountain!" blurted the guard. "It hasn't given water since our dear queen was alive! Did you know that only she could make it work?"

"Why, no!" said Jasmine with surprise.

"Many a queen," the guard went on, "has been wise and fair and even kind. But no one else has ever been able to get water from this fountain." And as the people bowed, the guard drew a silver key from his pocket.

The guard unlocked the chains barring the tower door. He led Jasmine up a staircase to a room high at the top. There, on a pedestal, bright enough to light the sky, sat the gleaming Star of Persia.

"Oh!" Jasmine exclaimed. "It's the most beautiful thing I've ever seen!"

"It is beautiful, isn't it?" said the guard.
"And I know how happy our queen would be to know it won't be
hidden any longer."

"What do you mean?" asked Jasmine.

"I mean," said the guard, "that you have proved yourself worthy,
Princess Jasmine, to call it your own."

"But how can I ever thank you?" Jasmine asked.

"By enjoying it," said the guard, "just as our queen did.
And promise to come visit us whenever you can."

"Oh, I will! I will!" exclaimed Jasmine.
And because she was not only wise, fair, and kind, but honest as well, she most certainly did.